Consumption
& Other Vices

Consumption

& Other Vices

A Novel

Tyler Dempsey

Death of Print

Published by Death of Print
wwww.deathofprint.press

ISBN: 978-1-0881-1349-3

Cover design by Tex Gresham
www.squeakypig.com

Typesetting by Zac Smith

WHAT STANDS OUT IS HER PUCKERED-UP LIPS. HER LIPS puckered, and it lifting like this. See this pen on your desk here. Just like this. A pen is where I hid the thing naughty girls like best.

Tonight, this night, of which we're talking, the night I brought over Jane. I knew she knew. Being from a wooded, hole-in-the-wall place, a place where roads curl like curlicues and people don't live in the large houses set way back in the woods—a girl like this brings company.

Does she get down. This is what I asked.

I asked and Jane and the girl, Clara, they looked at each other in the cab of my big brown truck. Giggling. She gets down is how Jane answered. They brought it to their lips and lifted.

And like this—I grinned and revved the engine. Leaves on the dirt road swirled. Me and Jane and Clara in my truck on a road where people don't live in large houses set way back in the woods. Good, is how I answered.

Don't worry, Jane said. She placed a palm on my oily jeans. You girls are going to get in trouble. They looked

1

at each other like two naughty robbers. You could be sisters, I said.

Giggling giggled by their puckered-up cheeks. There, in the cab of my big brown truck. As the roads straightened.

Roads that were dirt started being built with rock.

Houses, peopled with people houses, sit right up on roads like this.

It's like this—with dirt, and rock, with people with people houses. With types of roads, with houses, and how they're peopled—this is the way the road talks to me—puckered and whispering, like it does, to a person like me.

What it was telling me was that us, in the truck, were closer to Papa's house.

Where I live.

MONDAY. SUNSET.

Andrews crosscut by shadows of branches stretching over the field. His ears ringing. In the key of A-minor. That's new. Pheasants take flight through oranges and pinks, becoming dots on the horizon.

He saw nothing. There was nothing.

Nothing.

The Chase Bank. Two miles back. You see that, Shup?

Check to see if there's cameras.

Shupbert writes in a leather-bound.

Settling into the freshly turned dirt, the body lies facedown, arms a pretzel beneath.

Female.

A fly crawls in and out of her mouth. Stab wounds—forty-two. Victim One.

Warm. To memory.

LESS THAN TWENTY-FOUR HOURS AGO, SHE VIDEO-TEXTED Shaun. Fingernails painted at his house between flared hips. Shaun—late-shift—squatting with his phone out, pants down in the janitor's closet.

Fuck. What'd I do to you.

The victim's cell phone, caked in dirt, drops in a plastic bag being passed to forensics.

A radio is not heard above the commotion.

Forensics asks, How large a perimeter? Lifting measuring tape.

Andrews crouches. I'm not sure. What's this? Glitter? On her lower back. Hands. Forehead. Scanning as he talks. His breath mushrooms and plays off the blues and reds of emergency vehicles.

Sir, a perimeter?

From five feet away, Shupbert studies his partner.

The body considers life. In the ether, it merges with something.

Andrews' first and second finger rise. He tries to communicate. Quiet. Face-to-face with the body.

Sir?

Are you okay?

The radio. Requesting all available units.

Sixty-three stab wounds. Victim Two. He crawls to the other body. They tell you everything, don't you. He pets her hair.

The bodies converse. Over choices.

4

Goddammit, hands rising like birds. That bank—they have cameras?

A deer dissolves into orange mist. Against dry leaves, its hooves make a sound like *schewwech, schewwech.*

JOSEPH ANDREWS–DETECTIVE. PHILIP SHUPBERT–PARTNER.

The station of ringing phones, scraping chairs, whizzing bodies. The station reeking of fried bread. The station, always full, is empty. Eight days ago, Homicide of Lake Forest County moved two blocks down. Andrews and Shupbert did not. They stare at the map. Detectives who have not moved a cardboard box of things two blocks away. Here, for the stillness.

Andrews writes *Clara Hope* at the end of a line and runs it to one of two circles. Jane Escrow, below, to the other.

Phoned Jane-girl's mom. Not a typical Bloomington-type. Jane's groovy. Got this grown-up, in-the-moment, thing going, you know? Yadda-yadda. And—no. I don't know. Real talker. Something about her. Kind of sexy. Anyway. Point is, I was worried she'd know I was dozing off. Talking. Then, we got Clara-girl's mom. My god. Bonafide old-schoolers out here, huh? Between Bible verses and Lord Almighty's, she said nothing. Nothing valuable, anyway. Best friends since high school. Which I'd learned from Facebook. Plans on hitting the city after college. Yadda-yadda. Shaun Smith. Boyfriend of Jane, on-and-off since high school.

Smith? Questioned in the barn fire?

You got it.

Hm.

Was working, eyes paper, at Moe's. Night of the murder. So he says.

Diner north of town?

You got it.

Small towns. They're such nightmares. Postcard-perfect, but Dahmer's flipping omelets.

Alibi, or no—interesting texts from our groovy, in-the-moment gal. You get one guess—which night? His rap's...cleanish. Petty theft. With a few other kids. Families low-on-the-ladder. Joe? You alright? God. You look awful. Honest. Go home. Shave.

We aren't all prepubescent Mr. Rogers like you, Phil. Soon as you stop marrying twenty-somethings, you'll agree. No, you're right. I should see Louise. Call her for me? Have her get some steaks going?

I got my own to fry.

She likes you, though. Besides, I need a church.

I'm over you hillbillies. I'm going home. G'night, Joe.

The motel. Close to the Chase. The cockroach, or whatever. Have em start soaking the sheets.

ST. MARY'S. STAINED-GLASS.

He makes the sign, drops three bills in the box. He fingers the Santa Muerta figurine in his pocket.

The ear-ringing gaining steam.

A man sways on the sidewalk, strumming his guitar, Hoo-ly. Hallaloo-yee. Five dollars, peez.

He offers his final bill. Sorry.

Louise–

Dials Shupbert.

What? What? What?

Ever hear of the Interior Castle? Saint Teresa?

No. Goddammit.

How about the guy in high school? Know him?

Who?

The kid. Who would do anything for the throne?

Sure. Why?

I don't know.

CLOSE THE DOOR, I WHISPERED, LIKE THIS, AS THE GIRLS stepped out of the cab of my big brown truck. This night of which we're talking. This night I brought Jane and Clara to Papa's house.

Roads made of dirt that curl like curlicues where people don't live in large houses set way back in the woods, is where–from where us, and this truck, had come.

Papa's house sits up on a straight, built with rock road. Peopled with people houses sit right up on the roads like this. In this wooded, hole-in-the-wall place. Houses–where they sit, where a road is, relative to them, what they are made of–this is the way houses talk to us. Like they do.

They don't say one thing. One thing is not enough to say.

They say different things. To different people. Papa's house doesn't say what it says to me to other people. To other people, it says, Otherness, Rock. Rainbow, and Different.

But not me.

Close is the word, winding like wind through my hair, Papa's house says to me. Whispering, like it does, to a person like me.

Close.

Fuck yeah, we're going to get down, is what the two naughty robbers Jane and Clara said, looking at each other next to my big brown truck. Leaves in the air, by their puckered-up cheeks, swirled.

Both lifted the thing naughty girls like best to their lips. You girls are going to get in trouble.

At this, they looked at each other and giggled. You could be sisters, I said.

For these girls, Papa's house, seeing it and the other peopled with people houses. Having been whispered to by the road. These things made the girls lick up and down their puckered-up lips, and giggle.

Let's go inside, I said.

NICE.

Don't build em like this in town.

Imagine what something like this must cost.

They pass two deer and ascend the stairs, split the white columns, and knock on the door. The door opens and a woman emerges in a tank top and leggings. She embraces both men beneath their coats. Inhales.

Joe and Phil look at each other.

Come in, gentleman. Hand swishes the door.

Lavender, incense, and Bob Marley compete in the living room. She grabs a bong. Bends, hiding it behind the ottoman. Can I get you anything, her voice asks.

I'd love coffee, Andrews' eyebrows and thermos rise. You? Sweeps aside bangs.

Shupbert shakes his head, No thanks...Miss?

Escrow, Alise Escrow.

Pleased to meet you. Phil. This is my partner, Joe. You know—our condolences.

She opens her mouth and tongues her upper lip. Be right back.

Easy, Andrews whispers as she disappears from view.

Doesn't seem upset.

She doesn't—

Thanks, for like, taking the time. She turns down the volume on the player and puts Joe's thermos on the coaster and sits, lotus-style, on a pillow.

It's our job. Least we could do. Is Jane's father...?
Los Angeles. His throne in the hills.
I see.
He shipped us here. Jane and I. Two years back.
Bought you a house, he said. Don't want Jane having
access to the Hollywood things teenagers have access
to. Parting gift, I suppose. We were keeping it together
for her at this point. This was his way to give me the
country life I'd been nagging for and get his
responsibilities two-thousand miles away. To pursue his
vices.
Being—
Drugs. Fame. Women. A lot of women. Was hooked
on all of it.
So, Jane was—
Eighteen. Finished high school here and enrolled in
online courses. All I see is him in her. Like, all I envision
in this stretch is her moving out, finding a city, a man to
ruin her. No offense. Parenting is hard. Like I said on
the phone, she's an old soul. She'd say, Don't worry.
Got me into meditation. Cooled me off. I hated
Bloomington. Hated Don for abandoning us. That's how
I saw it. Jane, she...now, I appreciate what I've got. You
know? Don't think about what anyone else has. About
Don. His twenty-year-old with the tits. Looking like me,
twenty years ago. Phil's eyebrows rise. The real gift she
gave me. Almost like she knew I would need it. I
warned her about Shaun—
What about him?
Like sure, he's a sweet kid. You know? When you see
a high schooler and it's easy to picture them in diapers?

That's the type. There's something about him. Craves-acceptance-so-much-it'll-get-him-in-trouble thing going. Personality stable as a kite, you know? Just a feeling is all. Joe nods. Jane—she came to me. That night. I haven't told anybody. Up at three a.m., hounding the stations, nobody's talking. They're putting me on hold for hours. I'm under the blankets. Not even close to sleeping. All of a sudden, she walks in the door. Sits on the bed, where my feet are sticking out, and goes, You were right. I could see through her arms. I'm calm. All of a sudden. I ask this ghost of my daughter, was it him? Behind, there's a light. The whole time. Two men backlit. Their silhouettes. That's what I saw when I opened the door. You two, with the sun. It was the same thing.

WHERE'S THE BEDROOM, IS WHAT JANE, ONCE INSIDE PAPA'S house, asked of it. She placed a hand on my jeans.

Don't worry, she said.

I said, Clara.

I said, Jane.

Sisters, I said. You two are different.

They looked at each other and licked up and down their puckered-up lips. Like this. Together is where their lips went next in the threshold of Papa's house. Kissing is what these things made them do.

Where not all the outside is out, where not all the inside is in, is where they began giggling. At these things that happened.

It was how I looked. How I said it. Being in the threshold. These things made the girls do these things.

Here is how I said it. Look. This is how I looked when I said it.

Grown up ages, revving engines through this wooded hole-in-the-wall place. Tonight, this night, of which we're talking. The night I brought Jane and Clara to Papa's house I looked like I had never watched a wooded girl's hole-in-the-wall boots, like boots, rise into the cab of my big brown truck.

Like I knew nothing.

But I knew.

Jane. Clara. Grown up ages, in a place so deep in the woods, in houses set way back where roads curl like curlicues and people don't live in the large houses set way back in them. Girls, like these, are looking.

Like girls from there do.

I know what they're looking for.

It's in the bedroom, I said.

A STOVE'S LEGS RESEMBLE WAX, SLUMPING IN THE smoldering remains.

Think we'll find anything in there?

Oh sure, says Phil. After Alise's, I'm a little worried what we'll find.

Margie invites them in. Coffee? Something from the ice box?

Andrews wiggles his thermos.

The house smells like nothing moves. Shaun and Margie are motionless in the living room. Everything paisley. A Jesus Saves wind-chime dings by the window.

We'll start. This is a conversation. Alright? No one's accusing anyone. I want to get that out. We're talking.

Shaun. He's a good boy, detectives. Sam, he's the one. Kid suggested they rob that drugstore, so many years back. Magazines, candy bars, Lord almighty. It's all they took. They didn't hurt nobody.

Andrews raises his hand.

Kids, they do these things. Boredom. Angst. Means nothing. Most of the time. Grow up. Never slip up again. I'm gonna set this here. Doesn't mean anything. That's recording most of the time. Shaun, do you mind telling us what happened Sunday night?

I got off late. I'm a cook over at Moe's. He side-eyes the recorder. Old-timers. Come in Sundays. Leave church, crowd the bar. Down five-pound bags of

Folgers in under an hour, inhale their cheeseburgers, tip a few quarters. Anyway, thought maybe I'd grab Jane after I changed and showered. Wasn't sure though. Was tired. Coming home, I see flames from three blocks away. Over on A Street. You know how time slows down?

You could read by the light, Margie says.

Jane didn't drive?

Didn't have a car. Saving, she says—said. Said she was saving. We were gonna move to the city. Her and I. Once she was done with school, anyway. I loved her so much.

Andrews dangles a tissue below his nose. He sputters.

You didn't see her? Communicate at all that night?

I wanted to, like I said—Mrs. Escrow, she left these messages. I couldn't. Why'd they do it?

They?

They? Him? I don't know. Just saying, who'd even consider?

My son. He's tellin what he knows. Don't mean no disrespect, detectives. But we's hurtin. We want to know stuff too. Like who burnt our barn? Who killed a couple innocent girls? Fifty-four years. Never heard nothin like it. Our family's broken. Lord, almighty. Our family's—

Shaun. Mrs. Smith. Detective Shupbert and I, we apologize. We do. This is difficult. Nobody's saying otherwise. Say we take a breather? Think I could have more of that coffee?

She rises, You?

Shupbert shakes his head. Her dress lifts on a thermal as she enters the kitchen.

Shaun. You and Jane liked making movies, didn't you?

Palms rising, We didn't–don't tell mom.

Your mom–on the phone, she told us Jane worked at Hog Heaven, the ice cream shop, to pay off classes. We just talked with Ms. Escrow, and...

She worked at the sex shop outside of town, The Great American Bush Company and Fish & Tackle Supply. His voice a whisper.

The Gr–

Coffee, detective?

Andrews and Schupbert stand. They hover their cards over the table. Call if...anything. Ma'am. Shaun.

Phil trips over a dog toy in the yard. Interesting, he checks his phone, Boss?

Yup?

The cameras? They weren't on.

Goddammit.

Need a ride?

I'll walk.

Of course.

Two miles, Phil. See, the thing about small towns, they're just that. I'll call you. I want your opinions.

I hate talking and driving.

It's three miles. On practically deserted roads. You have plenty of time. Don't worry.

I hate you. He ducks in the sedan.

Andrews eyes the broken glass on the pavement. He phones Phil.

Yea?

His reaction. See it?

Something he isn't saying, you think? Fuck. These roads are windy.

Have our girls run em. Sam. Smith. All of em. However unlikely—see if the Department noticed anything when they were fighting flames. Maybe the shit has it in him.

You think?

I think we need to get him away from mom. I think nobody's story checks out as soon as you ask another person. Give it a day or two. Let the mind work on em. Then we'll invite Shaun for a chat. Till then, bug toxicology. I wanna know what they were on. What was that shit on her forehead? See if anything turned up when they bulldozed that field.

I'm at the interstate.

The Cockroach has another twin beside mine.

Andrews enters the Recreation Area. The roads become more and more river-like than grid-. He ascends a hill. A heron prepares for landing.

Louise. She wouldn't. Not without convincing. Too good. Maybe if I drop—

A station wagon crosses the yellow line, its tires half-in-the-grass, half-in-the-road. Idles by the recently-dozed field. Andrews ducks. Half a minute later it S-turns from view.

WHAT STANDS OUT IS HER HIPS RIPPLING FOR THE THING
naughty girls like best. Where is it, she asked, this night
of which we're talking. When Jane got down on her
knees. Where she got. Where she placed a palm on
my jeans and licked up and down her puckered-up lips.

Call me Papa, I said.

Papa's house was talking to me.

Whispering, like it does to a person like me.

This house, of which we are talking, talks. When Papa
lived here, this house didn't talk to Papa like it talked to
other people. To other people, it might say, Rainbow.
It might say, Different. What it said to Papa was
different.

Now Papa lives in the made-from-dirt dirt, where roads
curl like curlicues and people don't live in the large
houses set way back in the woods. Now that Papa lives
in the dirt, I'm Papa.

That's me.

It's the name people who are saying my name say.
Where is it, Papa, is how Jane said it.

When this house talks to me, it talks through me. Through my lips. Myself is not who I am when Papa's house talks through me. I'm Papa. Like Papa. Like Papa before him.

I was someone other than me, is what I'm saying. When Jane got down on her knees. When she puckered-up her lips on the oil of my jeans. When I looked through Clara—rippling her hips, giggling, like this.

You girls are going to get in trouble.

COUNTRY MUSIC NEXTDOOR. ANDREWS POUNDS. THE volume lowers, then rises.

What's wrong with me? A thermometer beeps in his lips. He googles *Why do I feel like someone else?*, toggling between that and a WebMD entry for ear ringing.

...hosting another person in your body... Jesus Christ, Ghost Hunter garbage at the top of my search? *Strong associations between ear ringing and early stroke...Christ.*

He swallows the Benadryl with bourbon. The thermometer reads 99.1.

Hm.

In bed. He crosses his eyes. His nose blurs and refocuses. Behind it, patterns on the ceiling resemble dogs from Hell.

He's on his back. Can't move. A figure stands by the bed. Made of nothing. But, made of something. It crawls up. The bed sinks. He inventories the long arms. Horns curving off the shoulders. It slides on top of him, the weight suffocating. Pushes his wrists in the mattress. Its lower-back lifts. The top of its head leverages his belly. Horns pierce where his scapula meets his humerus. He registers no pain. There's a window in the ceiling. Through it, he looks down on Jane and Alise, working in the grass. A voice from the room whispers, Look up. Its feet go through the window. Down. Faster. He tries to scream. His mouth doesn't open. The thing stomps. Long after they are mush, it stomps. It picks up Andrews, carries him to the parking lot, where there's a canyon. Its other side you cannot see. He's suspended over the rim, then dropped. Tumbling, repeatedly hitting rocks, he notices no bottom. His life plays out. Bones crack as he glances other rocks. He feels no pain. He slams bottom. Mostly dust and mush. But, his eyes see. He hears the whisper, now familiar Look up. In the void is a window. A man lies in bed. Perhaps, late-forties. Mexican. A look of manual labor. He looks at Andrews, looking. A figure, made of nothing, but, made of something, pulls itself into a headstand on the man's belly. Andrews tries to scream. His mouth doesn't open.

The bed's soaked. Clock reads 3 a.m. The fan, *squeak, squeak, squeaks* with his breathing.

His doorknob clicks. Hits the lock. Slowly, it returns to center.

Senses soar. He thumbs the hammer on his Beretta. It clicks. The maroon carpet grabs the soles of his feet as he moves across the room.

He swings the door, wide—cautiously, moving forward. The Beretta falls to his side. He looks on the lot. Lights flicker in a rhythmic pattern.

He turns. The map is blacked out. Bloomington County is the shape of a figure with horns curving off the shoulders. He blinks.

It was nothing.

Nothing.

THIS IS WHERE THE ENEMY WORKS.

Andrews over a graveyard of creamers, I'll hope for a second that's a reference to the stack of papers in front of you.

It's always the fuckin boyfriend.

Keep your voice down, Phil? These people just got baptized.

Bacon...Eggs!

It's Tuesday, for chrissake. You look worse, if that's possible.

I didn't sleep.

Cockroach not cuttin it? Too refined for its tastes?

Fucking tell me something already.

Want the good or the bad news?

Bacon...Eggs!

The bad.

Okay. Girls say the system's down. Federal contract-to-the-lowest-bidder bullshit. They can't run Sam. Or anybody. Not till IT finish their D & D game and get down to the command center to reset shit. Shuffle papers. Guys at the Department didn't notice anything, either. The skies were clear. And with an old barn like that, there weren't any wires. So, unless rats were boiling ramen, the thing was started. But, by whom, they don't know.

Andrews drops his face on the table. His arms and hands point up like, well?

The good news?

Toxicology.

He bolts upright. Leans in. What've you got?

Well, they haven't seen this exact compound. But the lab found traces of Clozapine, anti-schizo medication. So they think we're looking at something new. Tested positive for pot and MDMA. So, another designer thing, likely. Speedy-shit.

What do they mean—haven't seen this compound?

We've never seen it arranged like this, or what?

Like, they don't know what the shit they're holding in their hand is. Don't know if the glitter's, eyes left, then right, from here. Draws a circle in the air with his fork and knife.

Bacon...Eggs!

From here. Shup? Ever wonder what these skeletons—that guy—him, over there—what they think? Seeing kids in the same uniforms they wore when they didn't have a pot for pissing? Drooling over phones. Bartering over smoke breaks. Preaching happiness is owed them. If they could just find it... Think these farts want a do-over?

These kids? *These* ones? points fork around. The ones we see, day-in, day-out, swinging from their closets with their pants around their ankles? Taking the long nap in bathwater color of them barstools? Show me one happy person around the age of twenty and I'll pull my dick off. Those fossils are smug as us that it isn't them. Gotta leave, or blow their brains out. This dinged-up mug, how deliciously butter-soaked my toast is, day-in, day-out, represent something—sanity—

people, I mean, our species, moved past. Our foundation before we went nuts. What kids pine for is too abstract to understand. What's wild? Seems the degree of abstraction dictates the degree it controls em.

That's what I'm saying. Something else whispering at em. Ever think? This is gonna sound wild—ever think these towns everyone's leaving are jealous? Lowers voice, Like, they feel worship leaving, and there's a way for them to get in. Sneak into reality. Through a crack. And, try and stop it. And, the mugs, shabby storefronts, how the wheat blows driving out of town—once enough people see them, enough times, they become less and less an abstraction? What if, these—essences—I'm not saying they walk up, horns curving up off their shoulders. And in so many words—but, by getting through these cracks, infiltrating reality, what if, they, like, I don't know.

Bacon...Eggs!

Sure you're okay, Joe?

Right. What was the other good news?

That's it. Dozers turned jack in the field.

FINDING A THING YOU WOULD NOT THINK THAT YOU WOULD find—this happens to people in this wooded hole-in-the-wall place. Like other peopled with people houses that sit right up on the road is how Papa's house, to other people, looks. It looks like how I say it does. Like this.

What you find, walking into Papa's house, looks just like when I walk into the houses of other people. When from roads made of dirt that curl like curlicues set way back in the woods, girls step boots in the cab of my big brown truck—they might look like girls.

They might not look, these girls, like dirt. They might not look like roads. Or houses. Other people may not know these things live in these girls.

Whispering, like they do.

See this pen on your desk. A pen is where I hid the thing naughty girls like best. I flicked my hand and the cap flicked from this pen. Inside was something other than a pen. Inside, a pen is not the thing you would find. Standing. Up here, where I was standing—pen in hand, Jane, on her knees—I knew these things.

I tipped the pen. Where her lips and insides waited.

Like this.

Then I looked, way down. Inside her puckered-up lips. In her girl belly. The thing you would find was there. Swimming like a rainbow.

Like a rainbow Clara rippled her hips in the bedroom of Papa's house.

I heard my lips ask, of Clara, Does she get down.

Down, Clara got.

On her hands and knees.

Come to Papa, I whispered.

CHEESEBURGER...FRY!
Balancing plates on his forearm he glides past barstools. At the window, Your uncle was in earlier. Askin about you. Shaun slides a plate into Sam's hand. My uncle? I don't have an uncle, I don't think. I know you don't. Was the Feds, dummy. Wow, Shaun. What a wild kid—what—ten years ago? How is he now? Blah. Blah. Fuck's the Feds doing here? Asking me about you?
Fuck if I know.
You tell em?
No.
Serves the large family question-marked over the bar, the lady screams, Can I get them shakes on the sign outside?
Cheeseburger...Fry!
Outside this circle. We agreed. Now, Federales here? Talking shit about *used to be a wild kid?* The fuck?
Cheeseburger...Fry!
They came by.
The flattop hisses.
Why'm I hearing this?
After the fire. Standard—you know?
Askin about the fire, standard?
Mostly.

Mostly?

Bell above the door dings.

Welcome to Moe's, any seat. Sweeping hand.

What'd they say? Earlier?

Not much. In the door, first thing. Asked if you's working, I'm Margie's brother from out of state—Tom, some shit—was hoping I would catch Shaun with dinner plans.

I never mentioned your name. Or anyone's. They asked me where Jane worked.

Well. What the *fuck* did you say?

I told them. And, that I'd gone home. The fire. Nothing

You went straight home?

The spatula spins grease into artificial lawn rolls—spiraling them into the moat at the back of the flattop. Shaun swings bag after bag in the dumpster. Juices arc under streetlights.

He turns off the lights. Locks the doors.

Hinges pop and the Buick's cab alights. Smoke rises from the driver's window. Orange cartwheels into the parking lot and the tailpipe barks.

Andrews rises from the Cleaver's Hardware lot. He moves across the road. Lifting the ember to his nose, he inhales.

IN PAPA'S BEDROOM, I EMPTIED WHAT NAUGHTY GIRLS LIKE best into Jane's lips when Mama—hands by her puckered-up cheeks—stepped in. Where are your clothes, she said. You hole-in-the-wall kids.

I said, Mama.

Let's get dressed, she said.

She stepped boots to my box and flicked her hand. The box's lid opened, like this.

Mama's hips bent, and she looked, way down. When Mamas look—they look. When Mamas see, inside of things is what they see. Other people see outsides.

Not Mamas.

Mamas and Papas are different in this wooded hole-in-the-wall place. When Papas look, they see outsides. The road is all the road looks like to Papas. When Mamas listen, they hear leaves swirl by the made from dirt road, but not the road itself whispering.

But insides have nowhere to hide from Mamas.

What should you wear, Mama said, looking at Jane on her knees. What she saw made her giggle. She reached, and the inside of this box seemed different than how this box, on the outside, looked, while Mama reached her hand down inside.

Don't worry, she said.

What she brought up was like an apple. On the outside. It was round. Red, this thing.

On each of its sides, things hung. Like things do.

It was not a collar. But that, it also looked like, on the outside.

Mama walked with it to Jane.

She held each of its sides, this not a collar thing. In its middle, between Mama's hands, pressing Jane's puckered-up lips, this inside was not an apple thing pressed.

Open up, Mama said.

SAMUEL OLIVER PERNA–CLEAN–EXCEPT FOR THE DRUG-store. His eyebrows bounce like, *oh, oh,* the rabbit we're hunting.

I'm all ears.

Theft. Burglary. Yadda-yadda. Fucker shoves an empty hand in a paper bag at an Indian guy's face–says hand him the money or he's toast. Gotta admit, it's hilarious. Community service. Get this–four-years prior–investigated for arson. Went the way most investigations like that do. Meaning jack. Anyone who knew anything were certain, though. And Terry Allens. This guy. Sheet like a phone book. Christ. Joe...you there?

Any dads at home, by chance?

No, why?

Keep going.

Multiple battery. Multiple wives. Convenience store at gunpoint. Tried, as an adult, at seventeen. Three in County. Yadda-yadda. Sure you're okay?

Perna? Mexican?

Shup nods.

Older than the others?

He was our waiter. The one you lashed over creamers.

I'll-be-taking-care-of-you, Sam. Phil. Someone came by the motel at 3 a.m.

You didn't call? Jeez, Joe. Need more dicks? Party at La Cucaracha?

Hiding worms you deeper. No, they know more than us. We'll play the fool. What about Allens?

I mean, fucked up–Satanism. Talking black juju. Klan?

I don't know. Know I ain't gonna sleep for a week after digging around Facebook.

Think we can manufacture a warrant?

Doubtful.

Our boy–Shaun–is a pothead. I tailed him after work. Ten, fifteen minutes he spends at 307 Willow, then loops around. Takes his time. Making sure Margie's in bed. Toked in the parking lot after work, the fucker. Ballsy, given the erections local PD get over this shit. I think the barn was his post-work paradise. And, one night, he was careless with a roach.

Guess who's 307 Willow? Rhymes with Perna.

Motherfucker.

Hit the interstate early. You talk with Louise?

No.

Boss–

What's he drive? Allens?

Registered a '57 Ford wagon. Purchased from Gregory Allens, relative. For zero dollars.

Turquoise?

And white.

ONE-SIDED GLASS. SHAUN IN THE METAL CHAIR.
Doesn't look like he has it in him.
Looks like a toddler.
Shaun—detectives, Shupbert, Andrews. Nice seeing you again.
Nods head.
Preciate you coming in. We're recording. Chairs scraping. I wonder. Could you tell us a bit about Jane?
She was gorgeous—I mean—jealousy, big-time, when we started dating. Not shit changes here, you know? And suddenly a blonde from California strolls into English? People treated her like a trophy they'd won.
How you treated her?
No, I hated they went nuts over some arbitrary shit like where she was from. I gave her the cold shoulder.
How'd dating start, then?
Wasn't hard, you know, for her to spot her group. We dyed our hair, hid tacks in teachers' shoes, lot of effort to look different. Rebelling against our upbringing, you know? But for her, I think, she was leaning into it.
The first time you got together. Was it over on Willow Street?
Ashen.
Shaun, we know about the reefer. We know you don't want your mom knowing. Look at me. We don't care. We're not locals. I *could* call em. Have you

arrested. Or I could be silent about the whole thing. Up to you.

He breathes, smacks his lips.

We got high, by the bleachers, after lunch. I'm not like them—I swear to God. I mean, we've been friends forever—but, there were times, years would pass. Then, someone would land grass and pick up the phone. There we were, back in the routine, not missing a beat. I was an outlier, I guess. I'm friendly with everybody. Single-serve Shaun, Jane teased. Couldn't connect, on more than a few things. I didn't want to drift around, never fitting in, you know? But that's how it goes. To answer your question—we smoked, we found each other attractive. I think the cold shoulder helped, funny enough. We just...clicked.

Any prior relationships?

No one noticed me. No. Started getting more looks, though, once we got together.

Wanting what others have—is anything more human? What happened?

Felt like a million dollars, what happened. Believed I had a chance, you know? The line-cook at Moe's. Who shit his pants in fourth grade. Jane went on and on about getting away. How small-town labelling wouldn't exist. A city swallows that up. I didn't see an out, though. Our arguments circled money. I told her I have limitations. No way around it. She hatched this plan—I stay home, save rent. And by the time she's done with school, we have enough to go in on a place together. But—

She was more like my friends than me. I tried denying it. They were into harder stuff. I didn't judge. It just wasn't my thing—
Yeah—
Time's passing. And I'm not saving, you know? Not paying rent, but every time I check my account it's like nothing's happened. There's a threshold before saving's possible, I guess? Said it wasn't in the cards. She goes, Don't worry. Like it was nothing. She'd moved on. Starts spending more and more time with them, less and less with me. Snorting stuff I'm not into. I'm letting you go. That's how I phrased it—like, follow your dreams. She breaks down, crying. She's sorry, been distant. And gets this look, like *ding*, and goes, I know a way to get us out of here.

What popped for her?

We hadn't seen it—but, we'd heard of it—a drug. Something new. A few kids claimed to have tried it. Or had an uncle that had. They were calling it *Happy*. Supposed to be next-level stuff. I don't know. Her plan—get it. Then I could sell to her friends. You know? Since I wasn't in college, it would be harder to track, I guess? I agreed. Didn't think much of it. But, somehow, she lands this...glitter. That was another name for it.

Andrews hovers three inches above his chair.

She gets it, you know? But I chicken out. And have to work up the nerve to tell her. About a dream I had. How I was scared. But, by then, they'd taken it. Jane—they changed. Looks down, She started doing sex-work, with a coworker. Just for the cash, she said. Through this Facebook page, Swingers of Bloomington.

Mostly people paying to be dressed up and told they're naughty boys, or something. She seemed embarrassed. But we weren't really together at that point. Told her I didn't care.

Shaun, Andrews slides Jane's cell on the table, What's the video? Fourty...three texts mention it. In the hours leading up to Jane's death. Who has it? Promise it's not on your phone. Promise?

I got worried. These books on the occult start switching hands. And it stops feeling like fun, you know?

Sam, Terry, kill this dog.

Allens?

Nods, By the creek. We walk up on it, swinging. I told Jane I was through. She said, We can't do that. I asked, Why? They're all paranoid, you know? You don't want to piss them off, she said.

Or?

They wanted to hang out. A week later. Sunday. Something special they had planned.

Night of the murder.

Gowns, pentagrams. A Ouija board on floor. Terry, chanting through a voice distorter. Sam recording on his phone. That's what we walk in on. And—I can't stop laughing.

Exchange looks.

They dress her up. Put her on a table. Sam grabs my bicep. Kind of friendly, you know? But, like, restraining too. Alright, let them do their shit, I thought. Figured we'd leave once they made a point. Then her skin starts moving...like...a ripple on a lake. A vacuum, something, sucks her face. Or I don't know. Her eyes

shot from their sockets, man. And Terry's voice, it's getting louder. Jane's eyes stretching. Her mouth is...huge. This demon. Or a smudge. Like if you had glasses, and oil was on the lenses, blurring what you saw. Like a rip in reality or something. But I don't wear glasses. Then, a vacuum, something, sucks her face—
Sobbing.
Andrews drops to his chair.
Shupbert rubs Shaun's shoulder.
I killed her-er-er-er.
Worried looks.
Look, we're going to cut you loose. Where's—Sam?
Willow-ow.

JANE OPENED HER LIPS WHEN THE THING MAMA HELD ON ITS sides, when this smooth round thing, pressed. Like this. This night I brought Jane and Clara to Papa's house from roads made of dirt that curl like curlicues set way back in the woods.

Mama's hands met behind Jane's head. With look like collar things running through them. See—if she held them, like this, they look like a collar. Mama collared them together.

Fuck yeah, said Jane.

Mama looked inside Clara. Your clothes, she said.

Don't worry, she said next.

Mama stepped boots to my box. And reached, way down.

Inside, this box was different, than how it, on the outside, looked, as Mama reached her hand inside. In fact, what Mama pulled up was bigger than what, on the outside, this box was.

What she pulled up was a thing.

This thing.

Like clothes. But not.

Inside, Clara could have gotten, wearing the thing like clothes, Clara could do, which she began doing, there in Papa's bedroom.

Good, I whispered.

Mama looked. And with Clara inside, zippered the lips of this thing shut. Like this.

Like Papa's lips when he saw things different than Papa, things he saw ages ago in this wooded, hole-in-the-wall place. This, Papa's house began whispering to me about.

How before he lived down in the made-from-dirt dirt, on nights like these, when he lifted it to his lips, again and again, and his own Papa's Papa words swirled around Papa's puckered-up cheeks as he lifted it. And up into his arms we crawled, Mama and I. In his arms, us, together, we sang.

How his lips looked, then.

Is how Clara's lips looked when Mama zippered them shut.

SNOWING. IN DRIFTS.

Ankle-length coats move up the driveway. In the garage, Sam rolls from under a Chevy.

Samuel Oliver Perna—I'm detective Andrews. This is detective Shupbert. F.B.I.

What y'all want?

We're investigating the murders of Jane Escrow and Clara Hope. We have witness-testimony you possess evidence believed invaluable toward solving the investigation.

Fucking Smith. Pussy. I didn't kill her, if that's whatcha think.

We need to have a look. In case something hints who did.

Think it's Terry, dontcha?

Allens is a suspect. Along with you. Nothing personal.

He's a shit, for sure. Come on in, I'll letcha see. He spits in an oil pan. What choice I got, right?

Andrews and Shupbert sit. Distressing sounds issue from a cell phone. Lights from the screen move along the wall behind them.

Know what a burner phone is? Get one. Sam's cell dropping in a bag.

Fuck you.

Want to know a hack, Phil? Something I picked up? Shupbert grins. If you're trying to link someone—but, you're missing that piece. Sometimes you don't have to run it. Sometimes, he looks at Sam, it's a photo. Or a post on social media. It's their phones, Phil, you don't need anything else.

Phil writes in the leather-bound.

Sam? Want advice, so you don't end up like Terry, say? Say, you're trimming weed, they're face-to-face, say—you don't want to get caught. Wash. The fucking resin. Off your hands. Before you go masturbating to bestiality till dawn, or whatever you plan to do. Especially if you touch a rare, underground drug found on two dead bodies...

He turns the bag. It sparkles.

Wudn't me.

Of course, it wudn't. Well—in your familial opinion, does Terry have it in him?

The Pope fuck kids?

Excuse me?

A bear shit in the woods? He's the biggest psycho, here.

Andrews massages his neck. What did you make of that?

Some things, you— Shupbert's lips move, he gestures. Andrews looks confused.

Boss...you...can you...

Noise returning, Andrews supine, Schupbert stooped over.

I'm fine, goddammit. Calm down. Struggling. We go, tonight, get that warrant, bring everybody.

WHAT IS THIS, PAPA ASKED. WHEN, HAVING FUN ON THE BED, Jane held what looked like a phone in her hand, between her girl legs. Like this. When Mama whispered, You kids have fun, and left Papa's bedroom. This night of which we're talking. This night I brought Jane and Clara to Papa's house.

Jane's other hand—what it was doing—is what her phone was looking at.

Different are things Papa saw ages ago in this wooded hole-in-the-wall place. He'd never seen, in his ages, a girl, through the eyes of her phone, watch what her hand was doing.

Jane and Clara, two naughty robbers. They giggled. You could be sisters, I said.

It was Papa—not me, saying it.

Through my lips.

Different are things Papa saw ages ago in this wooded, hole-in-the-wall place.

Phones didn't whisper where roads curl like curlicues and people don't live in the large houses set way back
44

in the woods when Papa lived here. But—before Papa lived in the made-from-dirt dirt—whispering is a thing he heard them do.

Like they do.

Of where roads run straight, like roads. And, way up, the shiny walls of buildings crawl. Where people come and together talk and look up. But don't talk, or look up, together. Where—whether a person lives in air you can't breathe, or down in the made-from-dirt dirt—up is where you'll find them looking.

Singing it. Like a whisper. Like a rosary. Like wind.

Up.

DETECTIVES, 1:45 A.M.

Husband yells, Maria–Mama. Clinically deaf, sounds come through in tones, inflections.

Hair greased, Terry rolls the pamphlet grabbed when the detective raised the photo.

Poor girls, thinks Maria.

Age six–Maria resembled a gift wrapped in an orange blanket. Her salve, grandpa spurning deafness. From their window, she watches the sunset and landscapes running hill-like.

Terry shakes her arm, Zat right? He nods.

That right, ma'am?

Sweat frames Terry's eyes, blue, now black. German Shepherds pull police on ropes. *I should make a pot of coffee.*

At the table, the tall detective whispers to the clean-shaven one. Terry rolling the pamphlet. Drips sweat.

She is overtaken by memories.

What's her problem? Andrews gestures, palm flat.

Housekeeping. People going in, out, in, and out, laundry bags, holding their sins, accompany Maria on the bus. 64ᵗʰ Street laundromat. T.V.'s looping soaps. Magazines of large-breasted women.

Once she found a hundred-dollar bill, on a bed, folded to the size of a Tic-Tac.

At the kitchen table. The detective takes a stance, opposite husband, raises tape, Surveillance shows a '57 station wagon. Turquoise and white. Near where we found the body. Not a lot of white and turquoise wagons in Bloomington. We believe it's yours, Mr. Allens.

Aunt Griselda's German shepherd, Max. Maria's hands exploring his coat, fur lifting like dandelions. The detective lifts a mug with a picture of Goofy she got at Disney Land.

Her father opening Rosie's neck, with a dry rip. The barn smells of hay and life. Maria, on her knees, dress to mouth, eight years old. Old enough, father, to Maria's mother, Maria.

The next year, divorced. Feed too expensive, house too expensive, car...

Maria, at the kitchen table. Detectives levitate toward husband. We picked them up. 8 o'clock, Sunday, after drinks. *We?* Said, we was goin to the liquor store. Asked if they'd like to come along. His finger taps the table.

To save the foal. Shaky legs, afterbirth-slick, hay creasing Maria's face.

What happened? Detectives parallel the floor, three feet over the kitchen table. Open notebooks.

Maria's infant head dunked in horse's blood. Renewed by the Holy Spirit. Terry whispering, I have something for you. After bowling, ice cream in the wagon. A kid on a bike. Maria, screaming. In the side mirror, motionless, a tire spins.

To save the foal. Husband licks Rocky Road veining down his arm.

Maria, at the table. The scene—with detectives, the kitchen table—she's dreamt.

In horse's blood.

The detectives sit. Quiet. Ceased levitating. The clean-shaven one nods, they're nodding. In the kitchen.

The red hat spins on the hood of the car. A beautiful little hat.

SCOTCH POURING. ANDREWS BY THE MAP.
Who'd he mean? We picked them up? Connecting circles. *Sam? Must be.*
Yelling. Pounds wall, Keep it down. A man can't fucking think. Music rising in volume.
Tomorrow. Something he isn't saying.
In bed. Thinking of Willow. Fingering the Santa Muerta.
A knock.
He bolts upright. Blood pressure shoots. Beretta. Three feet, the door opens.
A four-by-four canvas bag. Fresh towels, linens. The girl, Maria, in a uniform, holds a note. We need to talk.

WHEN, INTO THE ARMS OF THE OTHER JANE AND CLARA crawled, and, down at their phones they looked, I knew. Being from a wooded hole-in-the-wall place, where roads curl like curlicues and people don't live in the large houses set way back in the woods–Mamas, of girls like these, live down in the dirt.

Mamas and Papas in this wooded, hole-in-the-wall place, are different.

Whether grown up ages on roads that curl like curlicues where people don't live in the large houses set way back in the woods or right up on a straight, built with rock road–Mamas, when they look–up is where they go.

The direction when, in their arms you crawl, both hearts reach.

Up.

Papas, where ages were grown, or which direction they look, matter not. Down is all they know.

You know, what keeps Mamas dirted to the made-from-dirt dirt, and not up, up in the air, like a rainbow.

I knew, this night of which we're talking.

When—gone was what we lifted to our lips. Gone was the thing naughty girls like best. Jane and Clara were the lips of Mamas in the made-from-dirt dirt.

Is what I'm saying.

When these Mamas, cradled in each other's arms, together, sang, and looked at their phones, and at me.

And said, Well.

I knew.

And raised my hand. Like this.

I said Clara.

I said, Jane—Sisters, I said.

Want to get down.

MARIA. AN INTERPRETER.

Andrews fills a thermos. Skipping the questions, was it Maria? I've shown you things we've shown nobody. You have the mic.

She begins signing. The interpreter's speaking, I know who you're looking for.

Clicks recorder.

I see things. They say if you lose one sense, you gain another. Growing up. A woman, a minority? Deaf, poor? Here? You look around. *He's not better than me. Sidnee gets boys, but why?* Isolated, invisible in my deafness, jotting my notes. On the various ways privilege works against people like me. Hate, jealousy, obsession. I felt it. Was raw with it. Close enough to taste what giving in would feel like. Luckily—I don't think anyone can do it—I have a brain you can trick with logic. This released me from that maze of thinking. Call it my religion. Are you religious, detective?

Something like it. He fingers the Santa Muerta.

Terry said, We picked them up. Talking about the girls. I love him—even the devil needs love. But I see things. Things that brought me here. A hit-and-run. A twelve-year-old boy. Look it up. Two years ago. Some things. Seeing them. Another you starts growing inside. And you have so long to turn it to smoke, before it outpaces, overtakes the person you are.

Have we? Met?

We picked them up. Terry knew the plants would get found when you searched the property. He's got a gambler's need to test how low the floor goes. He was home, Sunday, with me. Like I said. He's not innocent. Roy Rogers. That's the name. Look it up.

Did you come by my room? Did I dream you?

I have a brother. His name is Jose. Joe lifts from his seat. I think I was spared. Because I was deaf. But he never found that logic-key to save his brain. From the comparing. It was hard, watching your brother suck up to people he hated. He's what doctors labeled a true obsessive. It was compulsive, one thing, then on to the next. He never fit into how society's wired. So he sank into the fringes. Bizarre, sideways stuff. I don't understand it. To be frankly honest. But it might be that it's that sort of stuff that saved you.

Saved me?

Jose asked me, about you. It's where I work. He saw your car when you took the room. I found your Santa Muerta cleaning that first afternoon. You were out. He says the things talk to him. Maybe he heard it? If you say someone, or—something—came by your room? If that's the case? And—if Jose did what I think he did—he believes, and is ready to act on, someone taking your place. There's a law to the Old Way. Call it...logic? Do you believe? They aren't easy to find, you know? Where'd you get your figurine?

That's a story in itself. I earned it. Yes, I believe.

Well, you know, then. There are four archetypes. Combinations, repetitions of primal urges. Born, and recycled, infinitely. That's Creation. Both the act and what started it. If you believe. Certain combinations are normal. Others, not so much. After years out of the game, when they're born again, it sets off a chain of events. Your belief—that figurine. Might have reshaped the course of events. The bad news—it doesn't save anyone. Nothing subtracts, it just gets shuffled around. That's what holds the universe together. Or, the law it follows. Again, it's like an archetype steps through a threshold. And it's almost like nothing human's there. The archetype gets the whole stage. It sets off a chain of events—

How do you make something end, then?

Go to the beginning. After the first few words are down, the whole thing is locked into place. Jose's going to kill again. Go back to the beginning. It might not be the exact thing—but it'll rhyme. As the saying goes.

What makes you sure your brother's the one?

You found the girls, in the woods, on a dirt road, right?

Right.

That's significant.

Why?

He talks about them constantly. Detective? Looks at her interpreter, Should we call someone?

DOWN TO MY TRUCK IS WHERE—TONIGHT, THIS NIGHT, OF which we're talking, this night I brought over Jane and Clara to Papa's house—we went next. When gone was what we lifted to our lips. Gone the thing naughty girls like best. I looked at these sisters. And said, Want to get down.

Jane and Clara licked up, and down, their puckered-up lips.

Fuck yeah, they said.

Next to my big brown truck, leaves in the air—by their puckered-up cheeks—swirled.

Close the door, I whispered, as they stepped boots in my truck.

I grinned—and revved the engine, like this.

We're going to get down, Jane said.

Roads that were rock started being made with dirt. Houses, peopled with people houses, sit way back on roads like this. On roads like this, roads whisper.

Like they do.

This is what the road was whispering.

Where not all the outside isn't in, and not all the inside isn't not out, is where we, in this truck, were going. Where roads aren't too straight or curly, and persons not fully alive, and those not-all-too-dead—what is this word.

Where a person, not sure if they're looking through the eyes of their phone, or their own, decide they won't decide. Neither planted in a wooded, hole-in-the-wall place, nor anchored in the air you can't breathe— persons, such as these—hear life isn't what they show themselves, but a thing shown them.

It's what naughty girls like best.

SAINT JOSEPH'S. ROOM 3-B.

Smiling Louise, Asked the nurses for steak. They brought Jell-o.

Louise—bug.

Come to baby, opens arms. Bedside table moves. Cacophony of tubes.

Jeez, boss. You know—sitting here, with her. This whole time. And put two and two together. Can't believe you aren't together. Last week, I'm calling her, telling her get dinner going?

Enters room, He's awake?

How long was I down, doc? What was it? Stroke? How bad?

You hit the floor—noon, yesterday. And have been asleep since—looks at wall—6:30 p.m. the following evening.

Like, in a coma?

Like, asleep. You were severely dehydrated. Your body needed rest. We ran tests, there's nothing wrong with you. My guess? Stress. When was the last time you slept?

Saturday?

Shaking head, Sleep isn't to be taken lightly, Mr. Andrews. Your mind tried to kill you. Luckily, your body took over.

So—that's it?

That's it. But I wouldn't suggest the two of you, points to Louise, do anything. Not yet. We're going to keep you around tonight. Just in case. They can come get you in the morning.

Thanks, doctor.

So—yeah. Thanks for making me look like a dick, is what I'm saying.

Phil, I love you. But can we have some privacy?

Sure thing, boss.

Why'd you pick such a shitty motel? With your back?

Have to stay close. You know that. You get far off. On these things? There are too many rabbit holes. Getting into someone's head. Like building a radio. Except it's all mouse traps. They have to click, go off, a certain way. And the whole thing starts to whirr. If you find enough parts, arrange em a certain way, and concentrate, real hard—it's like, they'll whisper. Like, we exist out there, in a slipstream. We got a frequency. And anyone can just come along and pick up on our course, so to speak.

You're just like your father. You can't let a thing go. You act like it's almost mystical. Both of you do. Like it's the most important thing in the world. Whatever's going on in your head?

Nuh uh.

I hate when you say that.

I know.

She gets out of the hospital bed.

Angel? Say, we move here? And start over? Got birds you wouldn't believe.

My favorite bird's here.

His spirits drop.

You're going to die, Joe. You know it? You'll turn fifty-five, and you'll fall. Just like him. Quit this work, then call me. Okay?

I could see about maybe part time?

You fool. She laughs, They really don't fall far, do they? G'bye, Joe. She lifts a hand. Turns and doesn't look back.

G'bye, bird.

They don't fall far—go back, to the beginning.

Phil? Get in here.

From hallway to bedside, What is it, Joe? Everything alright?

Alise is in danger.

WHERE WE WERE IS WHERE PEOPLE, IN THIS WOODED, HOLE-in-the-wall place, go to live in the made-from-dirt dirt.

Town isn't far from here.

But it isn't close.

People can't hear what it is you're saying in this place. Is what I'm saying. Where is it, is what Jane, once here, asked of it. She placed a palm on my jeans.

I said, Jane.

After Papa led us to where he lives by our hands.

I said, This is where it is. And with this hand—see it—waved over the made-from-dirt dirt.

Jane and Clara got down.

On their knees.

And reached, way down.

The dirt didn't look like dirt when they reached their hands inside. When, up, the dirt went, in their girl lips. This night I brought Jane and Clara to Papa's house
60

from roads that curl like curlicues and people don't live in the large houses set way back in the woods.

Her lips, puckered-up, and it lifting, like this. This is what stands out.

When I took from my pocket the knife Papa gave me.

Like his Papa. Like his Papa before him.

And lifted it, like this.

They were not where they were. Jane and Clara. They were where a person—not sure if they're looking through the eyes of a phone, or their own—decide not to decide. They were where—neither planted in a wooded, hole-in-the-wall place, nor anchored in the air you can't breathe—rainbows sing in their bellies, rippling their lips like a prayer.

Look up, I said.

JOSE, FACE DOWN, IN THE METAL CHAIR.

Unbelievable. He was stepping out of his truck as the agents pulled up. How'd you know? I gotta know.

Call it a hunch. He said anything?

Only that he wants to talk to you. And that no one else can be in the room.

Not that he wants an attorney?

No.

Hm.

Andrews enters, Look at me.

Jose lifts his face. He grins, I know you.

Andrews steadies himself, You don't know me.

I know you. I saw you. You saw me.

Andrews ignores the figure standing behind Jose, horns curving by the ceiling.

We do know each other. You're right. But we don't. Really. We're adjacent parts of a puzzle. Archetypes. We fit, perfectly. Our boundaries don't overlap. For all the areas they touch. I hear you. You see me. We're practically mute—without the other. And yet. It's destined we destroy each other. And neither of us will learn a thing. And as we go down—there are others. Cropping up, on both sides, itching for our place.

Like this, he snaps.

Tell me everything, Andrews says, licking his lips.

Should we? End this thing? You, and I?

Let's end it. They're eye-to-eye. Tell me. That night? Everything that happened? What stands out?

Jose props feet on the table. Leans back, and looks away. For a while, he says nothing. Then, he looks at Joe.

What stands out is her puckered-up lips. Her lips, puckered up, and it lifting, like this.

Acknowledgements

This book wouldn't exist if Tyler Dillow hadn't seen a short story about a coffee-loving detective and said, I think this's a book. Thanks so much, dude. For having the same enthusiasm after what I handed you next didn't look or sound anything like the original. For making it look and sound better. Stu, who was going to publish before life got too big. And Alan, who stepped in afterward, saying he'd save it before he'd read it. For Liz and Ashley, who gave what every anxious writer needs when they have no idea what they've made. Zac, for reaching out now and again, making me believe I could come to you when the walls fell down. For being more of a friend than I deserve. And, for making the insides sexy. To the X-R-A-Y crew. To all the zines who originally published parts of this. Y'all rock. Tex. Thanks for the art, dude. And thanks to all of you.

Tyler Dempsey is the author of *Newspaper Drumsticks* (Book Merah) and *Time as a Sort of Enemy* (Gob Pile Press). He lives in Utah and hosts *Another Fucking Writing Podcast*.

DEATH OF PRINT

BOOKS THAT WON'T DIE

Deathofprint.press

The Ghost of Mile 43
One More Number
Francis Top's Grand Design
Drift,
by Craig Rodgers

Consumption and Other Vices,
by Tyler Dempsey

The Sun Still Shines on a Dog's Ass
Mere Malarkey
The War on Xmas, by Alan Good

Coming soon:
Awful People,
by Scott Mitchel May